GOOD D🐾G
11
Bo Hatches a Plan

by Cam Higgins

illustrated by Ariel Landy

LITTLE SIMON

New York   London   Toronto   Sydney   New Delhi

LITTLE SIMON
An imprint of Simon & Schuster Children's Publishing Division
1230 Avenue of the Americas, New York, New York 10020
First Little Simon paperback edition February 2024
Copyright © 2024 by Simon & Schuster, LLC
Also available in a Little Simon hardcover edition.
All rights reserved, including the right of reproduction in whole or in part in any form. LITTLE SIMON is a registered trademark of Simon & Schuster, LLC, and associated colophon is a trademark of Simon & Schuster, LLC.
Simon & Schuster: Celebrating 100 Years of Publishing in 2024
For information about special discounts for bulk purchases, please contact Simon & Schuster Special Sales at 1-866-506-1949 or business@simonandschuster.com. The Simon & Schuster Speakers Bureau can bring authors to your live event. For more information or to book an event contact the Simon & Schuster Speakers Bureau at 1-866-248-3049 or visit our website at www.simonspeakers.com.
Book designed by Brittany Fetcho
Series designed by Leslie Mechanic
Manufactured in the United States of America 0124 LAK
10 9 8 7 6 5 4 3 2 1
Library of Congress Cataloging-in-Publication Data
Names: Higgins, Cam, author. | Landy, Ariel, illustrator. | Title: Bo hatches a plan / by Cam Higgins ; illustrated by Ariel Landy. | Description: First Little Simon paperback edition. | New York : Little Simon, 2024. | Series: Good dog; book 11 | Audience: Ages 5–9. | Summary: As spring arrives on the Davis family farm, Bo is entrusted with guarding the chicken eggs, but his playtime with his friend Scrapper turns things eggs-tra challenging.
Identifiers: LCCN 2023028858 (print) | LCCN 2023028859 (ebook) | ISBN 9781665930758 (paperback) | ISBN 9781665930765 (hardcover) | ISBN 9781665930772 (ebook) | Subjects: CYAC: Dogs—Fiction. | Farm life—Fiction. | Responsibility—Fiction. | LCGFT: Animal fiction. | Novels. | Classification: LCC PZ7.1.H54497 Bo 2024 (print) | LCC PZ7.1.H54497 (ebook) | DDC [Fic]—dc23
LC record available at https://lccn.loc.gov/2023028858

CONTENTS

Adventure Jingles!

One sunny morning, I was stretched out on my favorite floor cushion in the Davis family's living room.

Not only was the sun warming my spot perfectly, but I was eating a bone filled with my most favorite treat: peanut butter.

Yum!

Sticky brown goop stuck to the fur all around my mouth, but the mess was worth it. Nothing, and I mean *nothing,* is better than a peanut butter–filled bone!

My human parents, Darnell and Jennica, know just which treats I love the most.

I was so busy with my messy peanut-butter treat that I almost didn't notice a funny sound.

But then I heard it again. *Jingle, jingle!*

Keys! It was the sound of jingling keys!

Like all good pups, I know this noise means that a new outdoor adventure is about to begin. I lifted my head, perked an ear, and waited.

Three . . . two . . . one . . .

"Bo!" my human brother, Wyatt, called out. "Want to come outside?"

His question was like music to my ears. It was as good as asking if I wanted a treat. The answer is always a barkin' *yes*!

After tucking my bone under the couch to save it for later, I quickly raced to the front door. I found Wyatt putting on his shoes. Imani, my human sister, was there too.

"Ready?" she asked.
I barked and spun in happy circles.
"Collar on?" Wyatt asked.

I lifted my chin and proudly showed off my collar. It has a shiny gold tag with my name on it. This tag means I have a home—and it's right here on the Davis farm. I live in the farmhouse with Wyatt, Imani, and their parents, Darnell and Jennica.

Lots of my animal friends live on the farm too. I'm so lucky to live with my friends *and* my family. It's the absolute best!

"Okay, let's go!" Imani pushed open the door, and the three of us stepped outside together.

There's something about running outdoors that never, ever gets old. Nothing feels better than a breeze blowing past my ears and ruffling my fur. Plus, the amazing smells go on forever and ever.

Suddenly a butterfly floated by, and I prepared for chase time! I was just about to follow it when I noticed Imani and Wyatt opening the chicken coop. I stopped and headed over to them instead.

Usually, the chickens cluck about inside the fence. But for some reason, now they were all gathered around outside the coop. They pecked and pushed, trying to see inside.

"What's going on?" I wondered aloud.

I hurried over to find out.

2

A Coop Mystery

I looked for Clucks, the head chicken, but she was nowhere to be seen. And I couldn't find Rufus, the head rooster, either. I finally made my way to right in front of the coop. There I saw Imani slip a notebook and pencil from her pocket.

"Bo, I need you to wait here and

stand guard," she told me. "Can you do that?"

I woofed my promise to do exactly as she asked.

Usually, the chickens don't like for just anyone to enter the coop. But Imani and Wyatt ducked inside anyways. Maybe I could try too!

I hurried over, but as soon as they stepped inside fully, the chickens filled in to block the doorway again.

I tried to peek past them without any luck. Just then, one of the tiny yellow chicks stopped by.

"Hey, Bo!" the chick squeaked. "Whatcha doing?"

"I'm standing guard," I told the chick. "But I don't know what I am protecting. It must be very important if Imani trusts me."

"It *is* very important! It's time for the New Hatch!" the chick chirped.

I had no clue what the New Hatch was, but I needed to find out. After all, I had a job to do! I am the farm pup.

"The New *what*?" I asked.

"The New Hatch!" another fluffy chick repeated. "You know—when the baby chicks come."

"I'll never forget when I hatched," the first chick sighed. "Well . . . actually, maybe I was a little too young to remember. But it feels like it was just yesterday!"

I had never really thought about where baby chicks came from. I'd always thought they popped out of the ground like flowers. They even *looked* like dandelions.

My tail began to wag. "*Woof!* I want to see! I want to see!"

"Good luck," another chick huffed.
"No one is even letting *us* in there."

Maybe the baby chicks couldn't go
inside the coop, but surely *I* could. If I
could herd sheep, Darnell and Jennica
might need me to herd baby chicks,
too!

"Excuse me. Excuse me. Guard pup coming through," I said as I squeezed my way through the clouds of feathers.

Finally my head popped between two chickens. I had a perfect view into the coop now.

I didn't see any baby chicks, though. Instead, Wyatt and Imani were just counting a bunch of eggs nestled in a bed of hay. Clucks was there too, watching as Imani counted.

She clucked as she counted along with Imani.

"There's a total of twelve eggs here," Imani said. She wrote it down in her notepad. "That's more than last time, Clucks!"

Clucks strutted proudly.

"Let's go tell Mom and Dad before they hatch," Wyatt suggested.

He and Imani ran out of the coop back to the house. I wanted to follow them, but I also *really* wanted to take a closer look at the eggs.

I squeezed and squished, and then I tumbled right into the coop and smacked into Clucks.

Poultry Panic

Feathers exploded around me as Clucks and the other chickens squawked in surprise.

Maybe they hadn't noticed me trying to get a glimpse.

Clucks did *not* look happy. She looked down at me with a sharp eye and an even sharper beak.

"Careful, Bo! What do you think you're doing?"

One thing about chickens: you don't want to upset them. Especially *this* one. Clucks is in charge of all the chickens on the farm.

I inched back, my belly low to the ground. "I'm sorry, I was just curious. . . ."

"You know what curiosity did to the cat," a chicken clucked behind me.

I didn't know, because I do not like to hang around cats.

"This is not the time or place to play games, Bo," Clucks said. "We are waiting for the New Hatch to begin."

I crawled a little closer to the eggs and sniffed. "You mean, the baby chicks are in *there*? But how do they fit?!"

"You fit in your dog bed, and they fit in their eggs," Clucks explained. Then she flapped her wings to usher me outside. "Now go, go, go!"

"I didn't mean to be a bother," I said, feeling bad.

Clucks sighed. "You're not a bother, Bo. But waiting for baby chicks is an exciting time. Like waiting for the first spring rain."

I looked around. Chickens paced back and forth, clucking quietly to each other.

In the corner of the chicken pen, two chicks fought over a tall pile of grain. "Hey! This grain is for the new chicks!"

"But I'm hungry now!" the other argued. "The new chicks will be hungry *later*."

A third chick appeared. "Actually, Clucks said this is *all* for me."

"I did not say that!" Clucks said.

But the chicks didn't listen. Suddenly a flock of chickens paraded past in a flurry of chatter.

"The eggs are taking too long to hatch!" one said.

"Nonsense," another added. "They are waiting for the right moment."

"I'm losing feathers over the wait!" a third chicken clucked.

Clucks ran a wing over her face. "See what I mean, Bo? If only I had the time to take the flock on a barn walk to help them calm down. But someone *must* keep an eye on those eggs."

I sat up tall and woofed. "I can do it! Imani asked me to stand guard."

You can always count on me to help! I always bring back Imani and Wyatt's sticks when they throw them. I help Darnell herd the sheep. And when my family accidentally drops food on the floor, I am always happy to help clean it up!

"No, no, no," Clucks insisted. "Dogs are not supposed to be inside the coop."

"MY GRAIN!" the chicks shouted by the feed pile.

"Oh, no! Oh my!" another chicken said, watching as two of her feathers floated down to the ground.

"Clucks, you can trust me. I promise there will be *zero* horsing around," I said. "Because I am not a horse."

"GRAAAAAAAAIN!" the very hungry chicks continued.

That was all Clucks needed to hear. "Oh, fine, fine, fine! I'll be back soon. Make sure *all* the eggs remain untouched. Promise?"

"I promise!" I said, saluting her with a paw.

Clucks ran off to gather the chicks and chickens, and then she led them out on a free-range barn walk.

Guard Pup Duty

I couldn't believe it. Clucks was letting *me* guard the coop all by myself!

Standing tall, I took my place right in the doorway of the coop.

"Don't worry, baby chicks! I mean, eggs," I said, peering at them. "You're safe with me. I am a trusty guard dog, and I will take good care of you."

I plopped down and stretched across the doorway. Nothing would get past me.

When a line of ants crawled over, I made sure they didn't come inside. The moment I heard a chirping cricket, I growled. Not a single tricky bug was going to sneak between my paws!

But it turned out that guarding was
kind of boring. There wasn't much to
do besides sit around.

I stuck my head outside the coop
and looked up at the sky.

Did you know that sometimes the clouds like to pretend to be different things? I saw one that looked like a bone, another that looked like a paw print, and even one that looked a little like my friend Zonks. Wait a second, that was no cloud—it *was* Zonks! He is my best piggy friend.

"Hey, Bo!" Zonks said. "Do you want to come to my pigpen? The mud is extra gooey today!"

"Oh boy, do I!" I barked, my tail wagging. But then I remembered my promise to Clucks. Slumping, I shook my head. "Sorry, Zonks. I actually have to stay here."

Zonks snorted. "That's okay! Have fun!"

Then Comet trotted over. "Hey, Bo!" she whinnied. "Do you want to have a race across the meadow?"

My paws practically itched at the idea of running through the cool, soft grass. But, no. I had made a promise, and a trusty guard dog always keeps his word.

"I have to keep watch over the eggs,
Comet. I can't race today," I sighed.
"Maybe next time!" Comet neighed.

I wished I could ask one of my friends to bring me my peanut-butter bone, but I was pretty sure Jennica wouldn't want any farm animals inside the house.

After walking in quick circles until I found the perfect resting spot, I made myself comfortable and rested my chin on the hay nest. Soon my eyes started to feel a little heavy. The air was warm, and the soothing breeze blowing through the coop doorway made me feel kind of sleepy. Maybe I could just take a quick nap. . . .

NO! I had to keep watch. I had an important job to do!

47

I paced back and forth staying awake and alert. I even counted all the eggs, just to make sure all twelve were still there. "One egg, two eggs, three eggs, four eggs, five eggs . . ."

WHOOSH!

Something brushed right past me. I turned around, but I couldn't see anything.

WHOOSH!

Whatever it was ran past me again, but I still didn't see anything!

"Hello?" I called out, a little nervous. "Clucks . . . are you back?"

WHOOSH! WHOOSH! WHOOSH!

The thing was moving so fast around me, it was a total blur.

"Why are you counting eggs?" a voice said from behind me.

5

Balancing Act

An intruder!

I turned around with a growl, ready to pounce.

But then I realized there wasn't an intruder. It was just my best puppy pal, Scrapper. He is a small dog, like I am, but he has short yellow fur. His tongue was hanging out of his mouth in a goofy grin as he panted.

"Scrapper, you scared me!" I barked.
"What are you doing in here?"

"I . . . have . . . the . . . PUPPY
ZOOMIES!" Scrapper hollered.

He started running in circles *inside* the coop! He rushed right past the eggs, nearly crashing into the nest.

Oh, no. This wasn't good. What had Clucks said about time and place?

"This is the time and place for that!" I said, trying to sound like her.

"Yay!" Scrapper zoomed back and forth. "LET'S RUN!"

I shook my head. "Wait, no! I meant this is *not* the time and place. Could you have the puppy zoomies a little later? Maybe outside?"

Scrapper tumbled over and looked at me upside down. "Bo, you *know* we can't control the zoomies. They just happen! And when they happen, A PUPPY HAS TO RUN!"

He was right. The zoomies are a bright, lightning-fast burst of happy energy. Every time I get out of the bath, I can't help but zip all over the house. Wyatt and Imani always try to catch me with a towel, but the zoomies are too powerful to be stopped.

"Why do you have the zoomies now?" I asked.

"Great question!" Scrapper was back on his paws. "I just learned a new trick. Want to see?"

I looked at the eggs. Didn't he understand I was very busy right now?

I groaned. "Scrapper, I—"

"Oh, please, please, please!" Scrapper looked at me with the biggest puppy eyes ever. He even whined. This usually only works on humans. But he got me good this time.

I wanted to be a good guard pup, but I also wanted to be a good *friend* pup.

"Okay." I sighed. "Show me your trick."

"*Woof!* Watch this!" Scrapper ran in fast circles around the coop. Then he stood on his back two legs. "Ta-da!"

A small white ball balanced on his nose.

Okay, I was very impressed. Where had that ball come from? I said, "Wow, that *is* a cool trick!"

"A magician never reveals his secrets. And for the final trick . . . good luck catching me!" Scrapper suddenly took off running out of the coop, the white ball in his mouth.

I woofed a laugh. Didn't he know I was working? I couldn't play chase!

Turning around, I went back to my guard pup duties.

"Are you still all here?" I asked the eggs. "One, two, three, four . . ."

I counted the eggs again. All eleven were there, safely nestled in the hay. *Phew!*

I rested my chin on one of the hay beds with a smile. Then my eyes popped open.

Wait a minute.

Eleven eggs?

That wasn't right. I counted again and again, trying to find the missing egg. Then I remembered how Scrapper had suddenly found a white ball.

My tail dropped. He hadn't taken a white ball; Scrapper had accidentally taken one of the eggs!

6

Pup-mergency!

This was a total, full-blown puppy emergency! I couldn't be a guard pup anymore. I had to be a detective pup!

Everyone knows a detective's best tool is his nose. I lowered mine to the hay and sniffed the eggs.

Whenever I need to find something, I always follow its scent.

Once I had learned the scent of the eggs, my nose led me outside the coop. But I stopped. I didn't want to leave—what if the chickens came back to find the eggs all alone? Would Clucks be mad at me?

She would be more *upset if she found out Scrapper took one of the eggs,* I thought.

So I followed the scent out to the other side of the fence. I looked all around for Scrapper, but he was nowhere to be found. This was *not* going to be easy.

My nose led me toward the pigpen. As I ran over there, I heard something following me.

Eeep! Eeep! Eeep!

Huh? Stopping, I turned to see what it was, but nothing was there. How strange!

Because I didn't have time to waste, I rushed over to Zonks. He was busy making the biggest mud pie ever.

"Hey, Zonks!" I barked. "Um, have you seen Scrapper? Has he stopped by?"

"He ran past not too long ago," Zonks said. Then he laughed. "Hey, I guess his trick *did* work."

"It worked a little too well," I grumbled. "Which way did he go?"

Zonks pointed toward the field where the horses grazed. "Ask Comet!"

"Thanks!" I zoomed off, calling over my shoulder, "Nice mud pie, by the way!"

I hurried over to the horses.

Eeep! Eeep! Eeep!

The tiny sound was back again! Still, I couldn't see a thing, so off to the horses I went. Comet galloped across the field, racing one of the ponies.

"Hi, Comet," I called. "Could you stop racing for a second?"

But Comet was faster than a shooting star. I barely caught her words as she zipped back and forth.

"Heya, Bo! What . . . is . . . up?" she neighed.

"Have you seen Scrapper around?" I asked.

Comet was a blur as she zigzagged back and forth. "Scrapper . . . is with . . . the barn cats!" She laughed. "Whoa . . . his trick . . . really . . . worked!"

I couldn't help but feel pretty confused. If Scrapper had performed his trick for Zonks and Comet, why were they acting like his trick hadn't worked until now?

"Thanks!" I shouted.

As much as I didn't want to, I *had* to go see the barn cats.

Hiss-direction

Diva and King are two of the grumpiest, sneakiest cats ever.

Most of the time, I try to avoid them. Now it seemed they might hold the solution to my problem.

I found the two of them lounging just outside the barn, tails flicking, as they sat on top of a barrel. When they saw me approaching, their golden eyes narrowed.

"Well, well, well," Diva said. "If it isn't the *sss*tinky Davis farm pup."

I lifted a paw to sniff it. "Stinky?"

"Dogs are always stinky to cats," King said.

"Well, I think you both smell *really* nice," I said. I figured it couldn't hurt to butter them up. After all, I needed their help.

"*Humph*." Diva hopped down and walked in a circle around me. "What do you want, *Bobo*?"

"Would you happen to know where Scrapper is?" I asked.

"Scrapper?" King asked. "I don't know who that is—do you, Diva?"

Diva sniffed, then waved a paw in front of her nose. "I'm afraid not!"

Now they were really messing with me. Of course they knew who Scrapper was!

"Please tell me," I said. "He has something super important, and it belongs to the chickens."

Now the cats smiled and narrowed their eyes, as though they had a secret they wouldn't share.

King asked, "This super-important thing . . . it wouldn't happen to be round, would it?"

I nodded.

"And white?" Diva meowed.

I nodded again.

"Oh, it wasn't the thing he used to perform his trick, was it?" King added.

Now my ears perked up. "That's exactly it!"

But then the cats shrugged. "Nope, we have no clue."

I slumped. Just as I was about to give up and head back to the chicken coop, Nanny Sheep came over. She is the kindest, fluffiest sheep ever!

"Bo, there you are!" she said. "Are you looking for Scrapper? He's playing with the lambs in the meadow."

"Thank you so much, Nanny Sheep!" I barked, then ran off toward where I knew the sheep liked to play.

"Good luck finding your stinky dog friend," King and Diva called out. "It seems like he's got a trick or two up his paws!"

The Truth Unburied

The sun was beginning to set by the time I found Scrapper.

He was with the lambs, just as Nanny Sheep had said, but he wasn't playing. He was taking a nap.

"Scrapper, Scrapper, wake up!" I said, nudging him with my nose. "Up!"

Scrapper opened one eye.

"Bo? What is it?"

"You have to give me back the egg!" I said.

"Egg? What are you talking about?" He yawned, then turned away. "Can we play pretend later? The puppy zoomies wiped me out."

Oh, no—when the zoomies finally go away, they usually leave a pup feeling super-duper tired. So dog-tired that it is impossible NOT to take a nap. But I didn't have time for Scrapper to sleep now.

I leaned down so that Scrapper and I were nose to nose. "Where is the ball you were playing with?"

Scrapper lifted a paw. "I buried it over there."

He'd buried the egg?! I found the hole covered with loose dirt and torn grass not too far away and quickly started digging. This caught my friend's attention and seemed to startle him awake. Scrapper quickly stood and joined me.

"Hey, you can't just unbury another dog's treasure!" he howled.

"It's not a treasure—it's an egg!" I shouted. I finally reached the familiar round object and very, very carefully rolled it out. "See? It's an—hey, wait a minute!"

The thing did not look like an egg. It looked like . . . an old *ball*? Scrapper's old ball!

He barked out a laugh. "You're acting super silly, Bo."

I sat back. "You mean, this whole time you had an actual ball?"

"Of course!" Scrapper said. "Pups don't need eggs."

"Then what was your trick?" I asked, tilting my head.

"The trick was to get you to leave the coop," he explained. "Zonks and Comet wanted you to play, so I said I would get you to come out. And it worked!"

I was so relieved, I laughed too! I hopped around. I howled. I even rolled over.

Cluck! Cluck! Cluck!

Uh-oh. I looked up to see the chickens heading back to the coop from their walk. Egg number twelve was still missing, and I had no idea where it was!

"I think I'd better get back to the coop," I said, my tail low. "I have some explaining to do."

"I'll go with you," Scrapper said. "If we hurry, we can get there first!"

9

A New Head

We ran right past the barn cats, past Comet, past Zonks.

Scrapper stayed by the coop door to watch for the chickens. "Hurry, Bo! They're on their way."

The eleven eggs I'd left behind were still there, at least. But I still couldn't explain how egg number twelve had gone missing without me noticing!

"I don't understand," I said. "Where could it have gone?"

Eeep! Eeep!

I frowned. "Scrapper, did you say something?"

Scrapper shook his head. "It wasn't me."

It was the same sound that had been following me.

Eeep! Eeep!

We looked at the eggs. They couldn't talk, could they?

Then Scrapper gasped and backed away. "Oh my goodness, Bo!"

"What? What?" I spun in circles, trying to figure out what he was looking at.

"You grew another head!" Scrapper said. "And it's wearing a hat!"

"Huh?" I looked to my left, then to my right, and I spun in a circle. But I couldn't see another head.

"It's tiny, fuzzy, and yellow, and it has a beak," Scrapper said.

EEEP! EEEP!

Wait a minute!

That's when, from the corner of my eye, I saw a tiny, fluffy yellow head. It was a baby chick, and it was sticking out from behind me! I jumped in surprise, which sent the baby chick scurrying for safety in the hay.

"Yikes!" Scrapper and I shouted.

Eeep! Eeep! Eeep! The baby chick hopped around the other eggs while wearing a white hat. Wait, no—it was the top of an eggshell!

"Wow!" Scrapper said. He came closer and sniffed. "This one looks younger than the other chicks. Bo, I didn't know you could grow baby chicks from your fur. Now *that's* a good magic trick."

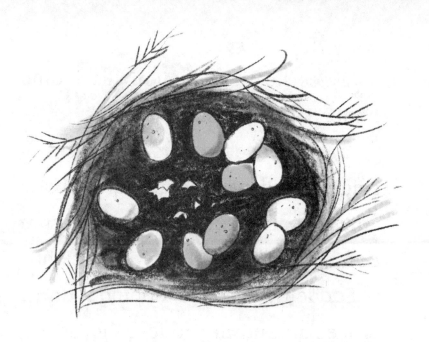

"This chick must've hatched earlier!" I said, peering into the nest. There was a small piece of white eggshell in the hay. "He must've hopped on my back without me noticing. This little chick *is* egg number twelve!"

"Does he think you're his mama hen?" Scrapper asked.

"I don't have feathers like Clucks," I said. "Or a beak."

Scrapper laughed loudly. "You sure don't. But that would be a fine sight!"

Suddenly I heard a tapping sound. I looked around and noticed that an egg beside the new chick was beginning to crack. Then another egg started cracking. Then another and another.

"I think you laughed too loud, Scrapper!" I said, lifting a paw over my eyes. "Now all the eggs are breaking!"

"What is going on in here?!" a voice
shrieked.

It was Clucks.

The New Hatch

Oh, no. Was I in trouble?

Scrapper and I turned around slowly to watch as Clucks and the chickens entered the coop. The hens gasped at the sight of the cracking eggs.

"I—I'm sorry!" I said. "We didn't mean any harm."

"Yeah, all the eggs started cracking out of the blue!" Scrapper added. "I didn't even laugh that loudly!"

But Clucks didn't look upset. In fact, she looked pleased. All the chickens stared in awe at the cracking eggs.

"Um, what's happening?" Scrapper whispered to me.

"Look, everybody!" one of the bigger chicks shouted excitedly. "The New Hatch is starting!"

We turned around. The chickens all crowded around us. One of the eggs cracked completely, and everyone drew in an excited breath. Something popped right out!

"It's a beak!" I cheered.

The little beak pushed right through the eggshell, and then a small feathered head popped out next. It was a baby chick! The new chick sat inside its shell for a moment, then took a wobbly step forward before falling on its tummy.

Something you need to know about baby chicks is that they're not very good at walking. But that's how most farm babies are, though. When I was a baby pup, I used to trip over my legs all the time.

More and more beaks burst out of the eggshells, and more itty-bitty chicks hopped out of the eggs and into the hay bed.

"They're so tiny!" Scrapper squealed.

Soon all the baby chicks began bouncing over to me! I tried backing away, but I bumped into the coop wall. The baby chicks gathered around me. They chirped and skipped, and it looked like they were getting snuggly!

"What should I do now?" I asked Clucks, worried.

Clucks smiled. "Just enjoy your first New Hatch, Bo!"

I looked back down at the baby chicks and gently licked one on its head.

Eeep! Eeep! Eeep!

My tail wagged. They liked me!

"Who gets to tell Darnell and Jennica?" one of the chickens asked.

Clucks winked at me. "I think our trusty watch pup, Bo, should have that honor!"

I woofed proudly.

Sit. Stay. Read.

Here are more GOOD DOG adventures!

GOOD D🐾G 1

Home Is Where the Heart Is

GOOD D🐾G 2

Raised in a Barn

GOOD D🐾G 3

Herd You Loud and Clear

GOOD D🐾G 4

Fireworks Night

GOOD D🐾G 5

The Swimming Hole

GOOD D🐾G 6

Life Is Good

GOOD D🐾G 7

Barnyard Buddies

GOOD D🐾G 8

Puppy Luck

GOOD D🐾G 9

Sweater Weather